an

illustrated by
Chris Rothero

AWARD PUBLICATIONS LIMITED

What an Alarm

In the village of Tickle there lived a dishonest little pixie. His name was Light-Fingers, and it was really astonishing the amount of things he took from other people without being seen.

He would take an apple from outside Dame Cherry's shop. He would take a biscuit from the tin in Mrs. Soap's store. He would pick flowers from old Dame Lucy's garden when she was out, and steal the pears from the big tree in Farmer Corn's orchard. And although everyone felt quite certain that it was Light-Fingers who was the thief, nobody ever managed to see him. He really was very clever.

ISBN 0-86163-734-8

What an Alarm first published in A Story Party at Green Hedges

This edition first published 1994 by Award Publications Limited,
Goodyear House, 52-56 Osnaburgh Street, London NW1 3NS

Printed in Italy

what you said should happen to a thief who wasn't cured by spanks,' said the watchmaker solemnly. 'You said he had better be sent to the Bad-Tempered Wizard. So BE CAREFUL!'

Light-Fingers *is* careful. He has been quite honest for a long time now, so perhaps he really is cured.

Tick-Tock took his clock back home, and everyone giggled when they thought of the trick they had played on Light-Fingers.

'And remember, pixie, just remember

And so Light-Fingers got the punishment he himself suggested, and dear me, he didn't like it at all, especially when it was Farmer Corn's turn, because his hand was simply enormous and dreadfully hard.

Light-Fingers began to tremble. 'I-I-d-d-don't remember,' he stammered.

But everyone else remembered, of course, 'Light-Fingers said one hard spank from everyone in the village!' a score of voices called out gleefully. Most of the people there had had things taken from them at sometime or other by Light-Fingers, so they were pleased to think they could give him one hard spank each. That would teach the bad pixie not to steal!

deep into Light-Fingers' pocket – and pulled out – his alarm clock, still gaily ringing for all it was worth.

'HO!' said Tick-Tock, in a terrible stern voice. 'HO! So that is where my beautiful green alarm clock went – into your pocket – where many other things have gone, I've no doubt. Light-Fingers, you are a little thief, a nasty horrid little thief. I am glad you said what the punishment for a little thief should be. Let me see – what was it?'

ringing,' said Tick-Tock. 'Have you a magic ringing spell?'

'No,' said Light-Fingers. 'And, anyway, I don't want you looking into my pockets. That's a nasty thing to do.'

But before he could stop Tick-Tock, the watch-maker had put his small hand

'It comes from your pocket,' said Tick-Tock, with such a stern look on his face that Light-Fingers suddenly felt frightened. 'WHAT have you got in your pocket?'

'N-n-n-nothing – except my red hanky,' stammered Light Fingers.

'Hankies don't ring like that,' said Tick-Tock.

'R-r-r-r-ring! R-r-r-ring!' went the alarm clock gaily. It seemed as if it would never stop!

'If you have nothing but your hanky in your pocket, let me see what it is that is

Then the market-clock struck twelve – and almost immediately afterwards the alarm clock went off loudly. My goodness, the noise it made! It had the loudest alarm of any clock in Tick-Tock's shop, and it made Light-Fingers almost jump out of his skin!

'R-r-r-r-ring! R-r-r-ring! R-r-r-ring!'

The alarm clock went off with a terrific noise. Everyone giggled. Light-Fingers jumped high into the air and clapped his hand to his pocket. Goodness! What could be happening?

'R-r-r-r-ring! R-r-r-ring!'

'What's that ringing? Where does the noise come from?' yelled Light-Fingers.

Now, as twelve o'clock drew nearer, everyone passed close to Light-Fingers, eager to hear the alarm clock go off. Light-Fingers couldn't imagine why the crowds seemed to be everywhere around him. He couldn't seem to get away from them.

'Good idea!' cried everyone. 'A very good idea. We agree with you, Light-Fingers.'

'I haven't seen it!' said Dame Lucy, and she turned to Light-Fingers. 'Have *you*?'

'Dear me, no,' said naughty Light-Fingers, untruthfully, 'If I *had* seen it, I would have taken it back to poor Tick-Tock at once.'

'I'm afraid someone must have stolen it,' said Tick-Tock, sadly. 'Light-Fingers, what do you think we ought to do to the thief, if we catch him?'

'Well, if anyone was horrid enough to steal your clock, they ought to be very well punished indeed,' said Light-Fingers. 'I think the thief ought to get one hard spank from everyone in the village. If that didn't cure him, then what about taking him to the Bad-Tempered Wizard. I'm sure *he* would cure anyone in no time!'

The market seemed very full that morning. Light-Fingers was quite surprised. People seemed to be whispering together, and nudging one another. He wondered what it was all about. But nobody told him. Nobody whispered to him that an alarm-clock was going off at twelve o'clock that morning, and that he, Light-Fingers, was going to get a terrible shock!

At eleven o'clock the town crier went round the market, ringing his bell and shouting loudly:

'Lost or stolen! A beautiful green clock from Tick-Tock's window-sill! Lost or stolen! A beautiful green clock from Tick-Tock's window-sill! Please bring to me at once if you have it!'

TOCK
GONE
OUT

So the next morning, when Light-Fingers passed by Tick-Tock's little shop, his sharp eyes saw a very fine green clock sitting by itself on the shop window-sill. Light-Fingers was surprised. Then he saw the notice on the door, 'GONE OUT', and his sharp eyes gleamed. He took a quick look round.

'There's nobody about at all,' he thought to himself. 'Not a soul! This *is* a bit of luck! And I've got my old suit on, too, with its big pockets! Hurrah! I can put the clock in nicely, and nobody will guess it is there, for I'll put my big red handkerchief over it.'

So in a flash the clock was in his pocket, with his red hanky draped over it. Then off to the market went Light-Fingers, whistling merrily. He thought he would be able to sell the clock for a lot of money when he went visiting in the next town.

'Now listen,' said Tick-Tock, with a smile. 'That clock is going to be an *alarm*-clock – *you* know, the kind that goes off and rings a bell very loudly at a certain time. Well, I shall set the alarm for twelve o'clock, and it will go off then, just when Light-Fingers is at the market. That will give him a shock – especially when I come up and demand my clock!'

'Now that *is* a good idea!' said every-one, pleased. 'We won't be anywhere about at all when Light-Fingers takes the clock; but we'll ALL be in the market at twelve o'clock!'

'But if we hide behind a bush to watch, he's sure to know,' said Farmer Corn. 'He's so very, very smart. He wouldn't take it unless he felt quite certain he wouldn't be seen and wouldn't be found out either.'

know how to catch him, because he's so clever. Can you think of a way?'

'Yes,' said Tick-Tock, after a moment. 'I think I can. Light-Fingers comes by my shop every day on his way to and from the market. I'll put a clock on my window-sill and a notice on my door that says 'GONE OUT.' And if Light-Fingers doesn't take that clock I'll eat my best Sunday hat!'

Tick-Tock, the watch-maker, came up at that moment. He was a little bent old fellow with eyes as bright as a bird's.

'Hello, Tick-Tock,' said Farmer Corn. 'Now just you use your brains and help us. We want to catch Light-Fingers and punish him for stealing. But we don't

'If only we could think of some way to catch him,' said Farmer Corn.

'I don't like accusing anyone of stealing unless I actually see them doing wrong with my own eyes,' said Dame Lucy.

'Quite right,' said Dame Cherry. 'We must never accuse anyone unless we can prove ourselves to be right. But dear me, how are we to prove ourselves right about naughty little Light-Fingers?'